Dear Parent,

Moving from being a nonreader to a reader is one of the most magical transitions in life. For some children, it happens with lightning speed. For others, more slowly. Whatever your child's experience may be, the best way to encourage reading ability is to focus on the enjoyment and fun of a story.

Here are some ways to support success:

In the beginning, read the story aloud a few times, with the child at your side. Be sure to read in character, to bring the words to life. If your child wants to participate in the initial reading, encourage him or her to do so. Run your finger under the text as you read to help the child connect printed and spoken words.

Let the child fill in words when you first read the book together, especially predictable or repeated phrases or words that complete rhymes.

The child using Level 2+ readers should have a good understanding of letter sounds and know common sight words. If he or she tries to sound out words when reading aloud, encourage the activity—but never force a child to struggle unduly with a word. Just say the word and move on with the story.

Whenever you read together, allow your child to linger on a page as long as he or she likes, examining the pictures or discussing the story with you.

When the child is ready, let him or her read the story aloud to you. Being able to demonstrate reading ability is an important part of learning to read.

As you read each book in the series, share—first and foremost—the excitement of the story. Realizing that reading is fun **is** the first step toward becoming a reader!

For Sam, Cassie, and Luke—
C.L.

For Roy, Robin, and Shawn—
J.H.

© 2002 Gruner + Jahr USA Publishing
All Rights Reserved. Produced under License
by Learning Horizons, Inc.

Parents Magazine and Play + Learn™
and Parents Magazine Tip™ are
Trademarks of Gruner + Jahr
USA Publishing Co., New York, NY

© 2002 Learning Horizons, Inc.
One American Road
Cleveland, Ohio 44144
Printed in Hong Kong

New Shoes

by Catherine Lukas
Illustrated by Jennifer Harney

A customer visited the shoe store one day.

"I need new shoes," she said.
"I need them right away."

"Oh, but Sir," she said,
"I want **special** shoes."

The salesman smiled.
"I have the perfect pair!
You can hardly find this
quality anywhere."

He showed her some loafers.
"But. . . ," she began to say,
when he jumped to his feet
and hurried away.

He soon came back with
a different shoe.

"Perhaps you prefer
a pair that's blue?"

10

"Sir!" she cried at last.
"Listen, please! The shoes that I
need look like none of these."

11

But the salesman did not listen.
He just talked away.
"We have this pair on sale today

12

"We have big puffy boots," he said, "for mud and snow!"

The customer rolled her eyes and said, "No, no, no."

15

She shook her head **NO**
as he showed each one.

The pile of boxes had grown quite high.

Then suddenly the customer sprang from her chair.

"Please be a dear and fetch them for me," said the customer excitedly. "Size 7, triple-E!"

23

"Do hurry!" she called.
"There's not a moment to lose!"
The salesman looked surprised,
but he fetched the shoes.

He helped her tie
them nice and tight.

She paid for the shoes,
then twirled around to go.
"Ta-ta!" she called. "Now it's. . .

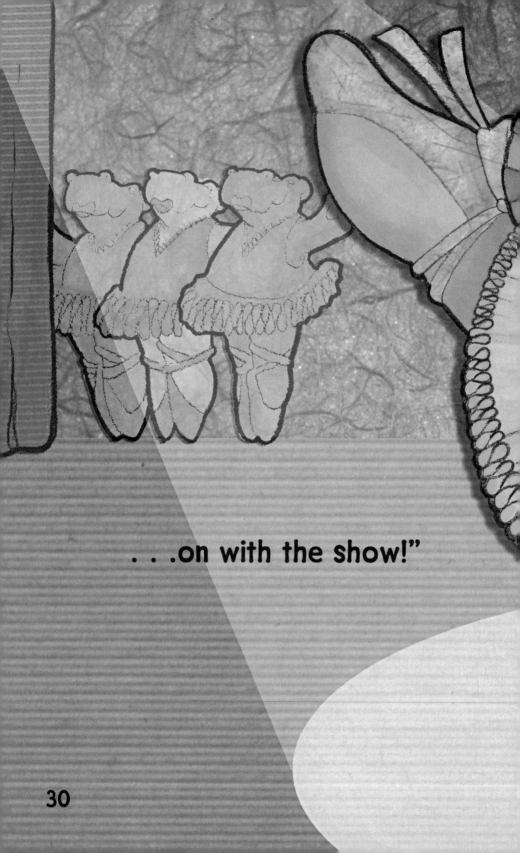

. . . .on with the show!"

Toe Shoes
size 7 EEE